TOP SECRET
TEACHER'S DRAWER

Poems, songs and silly stuff

by

PAUL COOKSON

&

STAN CULLIMORE

Cover illustration and design by Si Smith
Interior illustrations by Paul Cookson

All poems written by Paul Cookson & Stan Cullimore
All poems © Paul Cookson & Stan Cullimore

ISBN : 978-0-9933000-4-2

First published in 2016
by Caboodle Books

A Catalogue record for this book is available from the British Library.
Page Layout by Highlight Type Bureau Ltd, Bradford
Printed and bound by CPI Group (UK) Ltd, Croydon, CR0 4YY

The paper and board used in this book are natural recyclable products made
from wood grown in sustainable forests. The manufacturing processes
conform to the environmental regulations of the country of origin.

Caboodle Books Ltd.
Riversdale, 8 Rivock Avenue,
Steeton, BD20 6SA, UK.

This book is dedicated to

....

Contents

Introduction

Hello and welcome to our new book. In fact – our first book together.

Some of these pieces have been written as poems, some started as poems and then became songs, some started as songs and became poems and some just started.

We hope you enjoy performing these poems and songs.

They can be chanted, whispered, sung, shouted or roared ....

We might have our way of performing them but that's not the only way. Nor is it necessarily the right way. Feel free to edit them, change them, repeat favourite lines, try them in different orders, miss bits out, add your own bits - whatever you do - make them yours!

Poems and songs are dead while they are on the page - your job is to breathe them into life in the way you perform them.

Experiment with different voices, different rhythms, speeds, tone of voice - and see where the poems take you.

We may have written the poems and songs but if you've bought or borrowed (or even blagged) this book - they are now yours and it's up to you to keep them alive.

Whatever you do - have fun with the words!

All the best,

Paul and Stan

We are The Writers

We are readers, we are writers
We love to share the words that excite us

We are the writers.

Top Secret Teachers Drawer

It's a miracle of nature
A wonder of the world
How teachers can hide things
From every boy and girl
Chocolates and toffees
Popcorn and cakes
Sticky buns and biscuits
All get stashed away
The teachers hide them - for when they're feeling low
When they are feeling sad - they know just where to go...
      to the
            Top secret teachers drawer

You can open every cupboard door
You won't find what you're looking for
It does not exist any more...
      it's in the

                  Top secret teachers drawer

A mythical occurrence
Right here in school
Things hidden out of sight
Like they're invisible
Jellies and ice cream
Puddings and treats
Cans of coca cola
Enormous bags of sweets
The teachers hide them - for when they're feeling low
When they are feeling sad - they know just where to go...
      to the

            Top secret teachers drawer

You can open every cupboard door
You won't find what you're looking for
It does not exist any more...
      it's in the

            Top secret teachers drawer

A mystery of science
A magic to be feared
Things that go missing
Like they've simply disappeared
Sometimes it's children
That vanish from the class
Certain types of children
Such as ...
The girl who chattered all the time -
The boy who was a pain
They both got detention - and were never seen again..
   they were in the

    Top secret teachers drawer

You can open every cupboard door
You won't find what you're looking for
It does not exist any more...
  it's in the
    Top secret teachers drawer

Hey hey hey ! Call The RSPCA

It really is preposterous
To keep a pet rhinoceros
Cooped up in a cupboard in the shed
But it's not as rotten as
To keep a hippopotamus
Squashed and hiding under your sister's bed

It's not much of a laugh
To keep your pet giraffe
Downstairs in the cellar dark and hot
A python in the toilet
Surely can't enjoy it
Restricted and constricted in a knot

Hey hey hey. Call the RSPCA.
That's no place to keep a pet

It really is irrelevant
Where you leave an elephant
It's bound to make a fuss and cause a stink
And it really is bananas
To try and breed piranhas
Especially when they're in the kitchen sink

Do not leave your panda
Sitting out on the veranda
With a salamander and a stinky skunk
A porpoise will perspire
If it's in the tumble drier
And a porcupine won't help you play Kerplunk

Hey hey hey. Call the RSPCA.
That's no place to keep a pet

Mother's drawer for underwear
Is not fit for a polar bear
It's not fair, to leave it there at all
Don't ever keep an alligator
In an old refrigerator
Or behind a radiator wall

A buffalo will ruffle o,
The rubbish you have stuffed below
The tiny cupboard underneath the stair
An angry purple bummed baboon
If left inside your smallest room
Will leave it worse than Dad when he's been there

Hey hey hey. Call the RSPCA.
That's no place to keep a pet

Tricks to play on teachers

Trick No. 1 - for Sir...

Take some maggots
Add some ants
Put them in his cup
Take rats that are fried
Spiders that have died
To fill that cup right up
Chilli pepper
Makes it better
When it's time to stir
Add a snake
And it will make
A delicious cup of tea for Sir

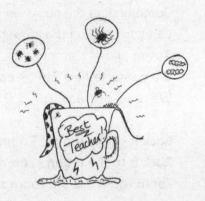

Tricks to play, tricks to play
Tricks to play on teachers
We were taught
Don't get caught
When you trick these creatures
It's lots of fun - for everyone
To see their frightened features

Rock it to the Moon

10 - 9 - 8 - 7 - 6 - 5 - 4 - 3 - 2 - 1 ... BLAST OFF

I was born on planet rock, deep in outer space
Come on feel the noise we make at every lunar base
Can you can feel the aftershock?   HEY.
As the planet starts to rock.   HEY.
We've started we can't stop.   HEY.
We're on our way, ...   1, 2, 3, 4

Rock it to the moon - Zoom!
Rock it to the moon - Zoom!
Zoom zoom a zoom zoom zoom

Rolling round the universe, you can see
Loud guitars and shooting stars rock the galaxy
Can you can feel the aftershock?   HEY.
As the planet starts to rock.   HEY.
We've started we can't stop.   HEY.
We're on our way, ...   1, 2, 3, 4

Rock it to the moon - Zoom!
Rock it to the moon - Zoom!
Zoom zoom a zoom zoom zoom

Can you can feel the aftershock?   HEY.
As the planet starts to rock.   HEY.
We've started we can't stop.   HEY.
We're on our way, ...   1, 2, 3, 4

Rock it to the moon - Zoom!
Rock it to the moon - Zoom!
Zoom zoom a zoom zoom zoom

Space Countdown Poem

10 - purple planets

9 - massive meteorites

8 - silver spaceships

7 - spinning satellites

6 - burning comets

5 - radar dishes

4 - shooting stars

3 - free wishes

2 - green aliens

and 1 little me ....

we're all blasting off to infinity!

Ukulele Mad

I'm ukelele crazy
Ukelele mad
Playing ukelele
Is the best fun I have had
I'm ukelele bonkers
Ukelele daft
I even play my ukulele.
When I'm in the bath

Playing ukulele
Stops me feeling blue
So I play my ukulele
When I'm on the loo.

I like to play it softly
Play it with my thumb
I play it with my fingers
Play it with my .... mum.

My wife doesn't like it
I play it every hour
She really isn't happy
When I play it in the shower
It gets her angry
Makes her see red
Cos I cuddle my ukulele
When I go to bed

Oh, me. Oh, my - can't tell you why
I'm just a ukulele guy.

T-Rex Rocks

A dinosaur party down by the lake
A rumble in the jungle starting to shake
A tremble in the air - like an earthquake
Cos everything stops.....
T Rex Rocks!

Heavy metal waves of heavy metal thunder
Dancing to the sound, of a rock'n'roll number
Brontosaurus breaks - into a rhumba
But everything stops ...
T Rex Rocks!

When the T Rex rocks – mountains crumble
Leaves all shake and tree tops tumble
Boulders roll, stones all rumble
When the T Rex rocks

A clickety click of his ten ton claws
The growl and the howl from his mighty jaws
The dinosaurs roar their wild applause
But everything stops ...
T Rex Rocks!

Dinosaurs stomp to the rock'n'roll sound
Pounding on the ground for miles around
Down and down - deeper and down
But everything stops ...
T Rex Rocks!

When the T Rex rocks – mountains crumble
Leaves all shake and tree tops tumble
Boulders roll, stones all rumble
When the T Rex rocks

A dinosaur party down by the lake
A rumble in the jungle starting to shake
A tremble in the air - like an earthquake
Cos everything stops.....
T Rex Rocks!

Does a poem have to rhyme?

Does a poem have to rhyme?
No, it doesn't. Not all the time.
You can have a rhyme,
In every line,
It's not a crime
But it does take time...
To find,
Lots of words
That rhyme

When you are a poet.
You make the rules
You break the rules
You can take the rules
And drop them in a dustbin

You can do
Whatever you want.
Isn't that brilliant?

So...

Does a poem have to rhyme?
No, it doesn't.
Not necessarily.

A Limerick about Stan

(written in class)

They call him Super Stan
He's such a marvellous man
He plays, he sings
Does crazy things
And I'm his biggest fan

Dad's Got A Duck

Dad's got a duck I've never seen
You can always tell where they have been
Every morning – loud and clear
The only sound that you can hear
    Quackety, quackety, quack

That duck must be rather crude
The noises that it makes are rather rude
Every morning – loud and clear
The only sound that we can hear
    Quackety, quackety, quack

It follows him wherever he walks, quacks and honks and
Squeaks and squawks
Every single step he takes, is followed by
The sound it makes

If Dad eats a plate of beans
That duck will always let off steam
You could end up in a coma
If you smell that ducks aroma
    Quackety, quackety, quack

If Dad eats some Brussels sprouts
Be careful what that beast lets out
You could end up in a coma
If you smell that ducks aroma
Quackety, quackety, quack

If he eats a plate of curry
Open all the windows - in a hurry
You could end up in a coma
If you smell that ducks aroma
Quackety, quackety, quack

It follows him wherever he walks, quacks and honks and
Squeaks and squawks
Every single step he takes, is followed by
The sound it makes
Quackety, quackety, quack

Invisible and deadly, it drives our family mad
The duck is just a stinky fib, the noises are just dad!

Going...

Quackety, quackety, quack

Teacher's Secrets

WHISPER - keep it quiet
WHISPER - don't cause a riot
WHISPER - not a peep
Secrets that the teachers keep

WHISPER - here's the truth
WHISPER - we found the proof
WHISPER - they're losing sleep
Secrets that the teachers keep

Last week
We sneaked
Into the staffroom
Had a peak
Guess what
It's got
It's the land
That time forgot

Just where
They're there
The secret cakes
That they won't share
The box
Those stocks
Of sweets and crisps
And lots of chocs

WHISPER - keep it quiet
WHISPER - don't cause a riot
WHISPER - not a peep
Secrets that the teachers keep

WHISPER - here's the truth
WHISPER - we found the proof
WHISPER - they're losing sleep
Secrets that the teachers keep

Maths is fine
We counted nine
Red, white and rosé
In a line
What's more
We saw
Bottles of brown
Behind the door

Facebook
We had a look
At all the photos
That they took
Oh yes!
We're not impressed
Teachers out in fancy dress

WHISPER - keep it quiet
WHISPER - don't cause a riot
WHISPER - not a peep
Secrets that the teachers keep

WHISPER - here's the truth
WHISPER - we found the proof
WHISPER - they're losing sleep
Secrets that the teachers keep

Uh - oh
Do not go
Into the cloakroom
On your own
You'll find
Disturbing signs
The PE shorts
They've left behind

Beware
What's there?
All these clothes
Behind the chair
Oh why?
A tie!
Who has boots
With heels that high?

29

WHISPER - keep it quiet
WHISPER - don't cause a riot
WHISPER - not a peep
Secrets that the teachers keep

WHISPER - here's the truth
WHISPER - we found the proof
WHISPER - they're losing sleep
Secrets that the teachers keep

Lots of random items
Lying all around
Some are on the shelves
Some are on the ground
Left on the floor
Where they put them down
You won't believe
All the things that we have found ...

WHISPER - keep it quiet
WHISPER - don't cause a riot
WHISPER - not a peep
Secrets that the teachers keep

WHISPER - here's the truth
WHISPER - we found the proof
WHISPER - they're losing sleep
Secrets that the teachers keep

ssh!

Tricks to play on teachers

Trick No. 2 - for Miss ...

Find her sandwich
In her bag
Then unwrap the foil
A slimy filling
Would make it thrilling
Add some worms and soil
Two fat slugs
Three big bugs
Can't leave it like this
One more filler
A caterpillar
Makes a super snack for Miss

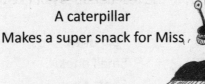

Tricks to play, tricks to play
Tricks to play on teachers
We were taught
Don't get caught
When you trick these creatures
It's lots of fun - for everyone
To see their frightened features

Teacher's Favourite Word

Every country
Round the world
Every boy
Every girl
Every school
Every day
You will hear
A teacher say

Bottoms, bottoms - children on your ... BOTTOMS

1, 2, 3, 4, get those bottoms on the floor.
5, 6, 7, 8, the teacher does not like to wait.

Big ones
Small ones
Short ones
Tall ones.
Shy ones
Proud ones
Quiet ones
Loud ones.

Every country
Round the world
Every boy
Every girl
Every school
Every day
You will hear
A teacher say

Bottoms, bottoms - children on your ... BOTTOMS

My Crazy Granny

I have a crazy granny
A very crazy granny.
I'm sure you will agree it is true
That my crazy granny
Is a very crazy granny
When I tell you all the things she likes to do

She juggles eggs with her toes
Plays football with her nose
And cleans her teeth with a cake
Wears wellies without socks
Keeps her hair in a box
And likes to skip with a snake.

We Are The Pirate Crew

We are the pirate crew
We ARGH... the pirate crew
We, (A-HA me hearties), are
the pirate crew
And this is what we do

yoho - yoho, yoho - yoho

There's Pirate Pete
He's not so sweet
He makes stinky cheese
With his bare feet

There's Pirate Mary
She's quite hairy
Got a bristly beard,
Which is a little bit scary

There's Pirate Ron
From Abingdon
He runs around
With nothing on

We are the pirate crew
We ARGH... the pirate crew
We, (A-HA me hearties), are the pirate crew
And this is what we do

Yoho - yoho, yoho - yoho

Pirate Jim
Is feeling grim
Cos a great big shark
Is eating him

Pirate Meg
Has a wooden leg
And a wooden parrot
On her wooden head

Pirate Keef
He's got no teef
Since he bit
The barrier reef

We are the pirate crew
We ARGH... the pirate crew
We, (A-HA me hearties), are the pirate crew
And this is what we do

Yoho - yoho, yoho - yoho

Grandad's Pants

Grandad's pants - old and mouldy
Grandad's pants - big and baggy
Grandad's pants - frayed and faded
Grandad's pants - creased and saggy

Grandad's pants - so embarrassing
Grandad's pants - what a sight
Grandad's pants - are a nightmare
Grandad's pants - what a fright

Grandad's pants - indestructible
Grandad's pants - gas and steam
Grandad's pants - very dangerous
Grandad's pants - clouds of green

Grandad's pants - secret weapons
Grandad's pants - won the war
Grandad's pants - they're explosive
Grandad's pants - please no more!

Grandad's pants - almost magical
Grandad's pants - a mystery
Grandad's pants - they'll go down
Grandad's pants - in history

Grandad's pants - so amazing
Grandad's pants - not forgotten
Grandad's pants - cover up
Grandad's pants - his spotty …. legs

Beware! Beware!
It's scary underwear

Milkshake For My Brother

My mum is totally brilliant
As a mum she can't be beaten
But when it comes to cooking
Her food just can't be eaten!

She gets bored with ordinary meals,
She wants something new.
Like crazy fresh ingredients
That she can use.

Once she found some cat food
Baked it in a pie
Then served it up for dinner
And made my brother cry

MOGGY PONG!

Then she made soil salad,
With stones, and grass and sticks
Shredded up with cactus spikes
It nearly made me sick

But today - the worst thing ever
All my fault, I think
She was digging in the garden
When I asked her for a drink

She offered to make milkshake
Like I'd never had before
With strawberries and milk
And something wriggly from the floor

She mixed it up and whisked it up
Nothing went to waste
She turned her back to get a glass
I got ready for a taste

Then my mother said something
It really made me squirm
She said the strawberry milk shake was ….
Made with wriggly worms!

I smiled and I nodded
As I listened to my mother
Then decided not to drink it myself
But to give it - to my brother.

Wish List
for your Brother or Sister

(when they're annoying)

I wish you nasty illnesses
Like spots and chicken pox

I wish you nasty surprises
Like spiders in your socks

I wish that you were locked inside
The snake cage at the zoo

I wish our dog had diarrhoea
In your favourite shoe

I wish your fingers were sausages
And a lion bit them off

I wish you swallowed a cockroach
And it made you cough

I wish when you went swimming
A shark was in the pool

I wish your head exploded
That would be so cool

I wish you drank some slug juice
And worms wee-ed in your hair

I wish you had wasps in your underpants
To sting you - everywhere

When mum was having a baby
This is what I said,
"I don't want a brother or a sister,
Can I please have a puppy instead?"

Aunts don't dance

There's one thing you should not do
Leave your aunts in public view
Do not give your aunties half a chance
They'll embarrass you when they dance

Cos she'll look just like a crazy kangaroo
A cockatoo that needs the loo
A bungee jumping chimpanzee
Or a weird waltzing wallaby

A...... U ..... N .... T .... Y ....
A - U - N - T - Why?
A - U - N - T - Why?
A - U - N - T - Why?
Why oh why, why oh why?

Do not let your auntie do the jive
Like a slippy snake she'll writhe
She will wiggle, turn and twist
She is such an exhibitionist

She twitches like an itchy grizzly bear
Like there's pepper in her underwear
The daft expression on her face
Looks like she's from outer space

A...... U ..... N .... T .... Y ....
A - U - N - T - Why?
A - U - N - T - Why?
A - U - N - T - Why?
Why oh why, why oh why?

Now we're going to give you all a chance
Let's all do the crazy Aunty dance
Move just like there's ants in your pants
Crazy ants dancing in your pants

Wave your arms like crazy in the air
Wave your arms everywhere
Now move your head and shake your hair
Shake your hair like you don't care

A...... U ..... N .... T .... Y ....
A - U - N - T - Why?
A - U - N - T - Why?
A - U - N - T - Why?
Why oh why, why oh why?

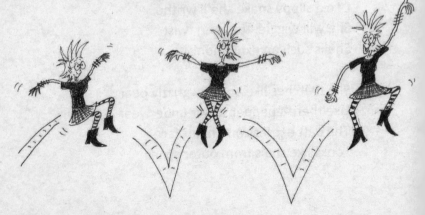

Naughty Uncle Norman

Naughty Uncle Norman
Is as cool as ice
Naughty Uncle Norman
Is naughty but very nice

Naughty Uncle Norman never works, he only plays
This is what, Naughty Uncle Norman always says...

A nose is for picking
A knife is for licking
A fork is for flicking your food
A jelly is for slurping
A fizzy drink is for burping
A song is for singing, if it's rude

Naughty Uncle Norman never works, he only plays
This is what, Naughty Uncle Norman always says...

A tongue is for blowing
Water is for throwing
At brothers or sisters who drive you mad
Bedtime is sweet time
Chocolate and treat time
Life is too short to be sad

RASP!

Naughty Uncle Norman
Doesn't make you clean your teeth
Doesn't make you brush your hair
Doesn't make you tidy your bedroom
Doesn't seem to care...
If you shout or scream (or even if you swear)

Naughty Uncle Norman
Is as cool as ice
And all my children think
That he, is really rather nice

Another Limerick about Stan

(written in class)

They call him silly Stan
He's a weird and crazy man
He is so very old
He's covered in mould
Like a putrid Peter Pan

What's Going on With Mr Wolf?

When the moon is getting fuller
And the nights are getting duller
Our teacher changes colour
Full moon nightmare scary
You'd better all be wary
He gets wiry and gets hairy

What's going on with Mr Wolf?

Bloodshot eyes start staring
Nostrils they start flaring
Trousers they start tearing
He's grunting and he's munching
He's growling and he's crunching
Soon he will lunching.

What's going on with Mr Wolf?

First he licked his lips
Then he started with year 6
Ripped year 5 to bits
Now he's wanting more
Watch out - year 4
Better lock your classroom door

What's going on with Mr Wolf?

Year 3 and Year 2,
He's coming after you
And what will Year 1 do?
There's a way to beat this creature
The one who wants to eat ya
Feed him your head teacher.

*What's going on with Mr
Woooooooooooooooooooooooooolf?*

The Cuddly Monster

8 friendly eyes

5 fluffy toes

6 pink tails

1 button nose

Scary Monster

3 bloodshot eyes

2 scaly jaws

4 enormous warts

7 red claws

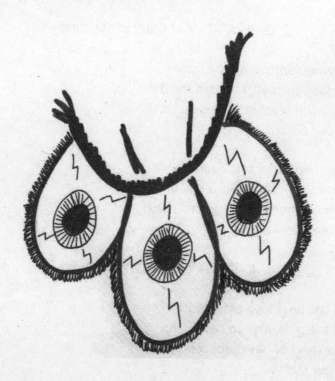

Crazy in Our Class

All the girls, all the boys
Run around, making noise
The teacher plays, with all the toys
In our class ...

Girls are giggling like they do
The boys are making a bogey zoo
The teacher's face is turning blue
In our class ...

C - R - A - Z - Y ?   Crazy in our class

Playing football on the floor
Kicking the ball, through the door
Now the teacher's keeping score
In our class ...

Boys are bouncing, everywhere
All the girls, have purple hair,
The teacher's dancing on a chair
In our class...

C - R - A - Z - Y ?   Crazy in our class

All the boys love extra work
All the girls, love to twerk
The teacher hates doing homework
In our class ...

You can hear us in the hall
We're the craziest class of all
We make the teacher climb the wall
In our class ...

C - R - A - Z - Y ? Crazy in our class.

Nonsense, Nonsense

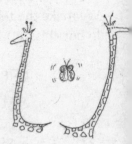

Cross your heart, hope to die
Two giraffes and a butterfly

One potato, two potato, three potato, four
Spiders on the ceiling, spiders on the floor

Round and round in circles like a teddy bear
Oh no, where did it go? I've lost my underwear

Humpty, Dumpty, what a numpty!
He was round and he was small
He closed his eyes - and tried to fly
That's why he fell off the wall!

Cross your heart, hope to die
I spy a teacher, eating a pie

One potato, two potato, three potato four
Nonsense, nonsense – please no more!

My Mother is a Chocolate Lover

Watch out! Beware
Don't touch that chocolate éclair
I wouldn't risk it
Don't touch that chocolate biscuit

Cos if we're good and we do what we should -
My mum will be quite gentle
But cross the line and we will find -
That gentle mum gets temperamental

N - O, spells no - don't go too far
N - O, spells no - leave that chocolate bar

Because my mother
Is a chocolate lover
Touch her stuff
And she'll rip your head right off

For goodness sake
Don't touch that chocolate cake
You'll get hurt,
If you touch that dessert

If we're good and we do what we should -
My mum will be quite gentle
But cross the line and we will find -
That gentle mum gets temperamental

N - O, spells no - don't go too far
N - O, spells no - leave that chocolate bar

Because my mother
Is a chocolate lover
Touch her stuff
And she'll rip your head right off

Once I did it,
I stole all her chocs
Mum went crazy
Nearly blew her top

We all know that in times like these -
When your mum's as mad as a frog.
It's every one for themselves and so -
I told her that the chocolate thief was the dog

N - O, spells no - don't go too far
N - O, spells no - leave that chocolate bar

Because my mother
Is a chocolate lover
She picked up the dog
And she ripped its head right off

Because my mother
Is a chocolate lover.

Mathematical, Telepathical, Mostly Magical Miracle

There's a mathematical, telepathical, mostly magical,
miracle
That works with any number from one right up to ten

Think of a number, from one to ten
Any one will do
Are you ready with your number?
Then multiply the number by two

Once you have this answer
Simply add on six
When you've got this new total
Here's what you do next ...

Halve the total that you have got
(This is the magical mystery)
Subtract the number you started
with
And your answer will be ... 3

It's a mathematical, telepathical, mostly magical, miracle
And it works with any number from one right up to ....
Infinity

Bicycle

I love to ride
My bicycle
I love the way
It makes me feel

Got two wheels
Got a bell
Got a seat
Brakes as well

I pedal fast
I pedal slow
The faster I pedal
The faster I go

I Didn't Paint the Goldfish Blue

I may have broken mum's best vase
And flushed her flowers down the loo
I may have eaten my brothers birthday cake
And stolen my sisters roller skates
But I tell you there has been a mistake
I didn't paint the goldfish blue

I may have smeared the toilet seat
With lots of superglue
I may have helped some sweets to disappear
And shouted "aargh!" in my granny's ear
But say it loud and say it clear
I didn't paint the goldfish blue

It's true, it's true, I didn't paint the goldfish blue

I may have sneezed into the saucepan
When mum was making a stew
I may have burped on cousin Finn
Put the baby in the rubbish bin
Let me say it loud, just one more thing
I didn't paint the goldfish blue

I might have shaved next door's cat
And cuddled their cockatoo
I may have been there
When they found a whoopee cushion
on my teachers chair
But I hereby promise and I do declare
I didn't paint the goldfish blue

It's true, it's true, I didn't paint the goldfish blue

Red and orange and yellow and green
Indigo and violet too
I may have painted the goldfish all those colours ... but
I didn't paint the goldfish blue

You see, I wanted a rainbow fish
So there was only one thing to do
I painted his tail, I painted his head
I thought he would love it, but then instead
My goldfish ended up ... quite dead
And then his body went blue

It's true, it's true, and then his body went blue
(He died)
It's true, it's true, and then his body went blue
(And I flushed him down the loo)
It's true, it's true, I flushed him down the loo

BUT - I didn't paint the goldfish blue.

Mrs Radar's Ears

The clicking of fingers
The bouncing of a ball
The distant squeak of trainers
Running round the hall
The lunch ladies shouting
The opening of cans
The dripping of the taps
The clapping of hands

One teacher hears it all
From the classroom to the hall...

Beep Beep Beep – everything she hears
Beep beep beep – Mrs Radar's ears
Beep beep beep – everything she hears
Beep, beep, beep - Mrs Radar's ears

The crunching of crisps
The dropping of a pin
The rustling of papers
Thrown into the bin
The scratching of pencils
The creaking of the chairs
The answers that are whispered
Footsteps on the stairs

One teacher hears it all
From the classroom to the hall...

Beep Beep Beep – everything she hears
Beep beep beep – Mrs Radar's ears
Beep beep beep – everything she hears
Beep, beep, beep - Mrs Radar's ears

The fizzing of pop
Every tiny slurp
The sounds of secret sipping
Every tiny burp
Every cheer at football
Every hiss and boo
Any boy or girl
When they go to the loo.

One teacher hears it all,
From the classroom to the hall…

Beep Beep Beep – everything she hears
Beep beep beep – Mrs Radar's ears
Beep beep beep – everything she hears
Beep, beep, beep - Mrs Radar's ears

Breakfast

I love breakfast time
If you want I'll tell you why
I love breakfast time
Cos that's when I eat my breakfast

Which happens to be

Snails on toast ...

With worms

My Dog is Dead

A python bit my brother
I found a rhino in the shed
The alien in mum's closet
Put a king prawn in my bed

My dog is dead
And so's the cat
Yesterday my goldfish drowned
And my rabbit had a heart attack

There's a panda in my pocket
And my turtle is turning pink
I found spiders in my socks
And a hamster in the sink

My dog is dead
And so's the cat
Yesterday my goldfish drowned
And my rabbit had a heart attack

Sigh -

It really hasn't been a good week for my pets!

Football Counting

I kicked my ball

1 - against the wall
2 - in the bathroom
3 - in the hall
4 - in the kitchen
5 - at the door
6 - at my sister
7 - times more
8 - at the gate
9 - at the slide
10 - at the greenhouse

Then I had to hide
Crash, bang, tinkle, wallop - then I had to hide

I kicked my ball

11 - on my bed
12 - at the garage
13 - at the shed
14 - at the dog
15 - at the cat

16 - at my granny (knocked off her hat)
17 - at the hedge
18 - on the grass
19 - at the window
20 - at the glass

Then I ran away so fast,
Crash, bang, tinkle, wallop - then I ran away so fast

CRASH, BANG, TINKLE, WALLOP!

Martian Maths

Maths on Mars, is easy and never hard.
Maths on Mars is easy peasy...

Martian maths - Martian maths
Martian maths... is totally daft
Martian maths - Martian maths
Martian mathematics...

1 plus 1 is 9,
9 times 3 is 4
4 times a brussel sprout
Is a carrot, on the floor (or more)

5 times 6 is a lot
6 times 9 isn't fair
9 divided by bagpipes
Is curly ginger hair (in the air)

Martian maths - Martian maths
Martian maths... is totally daft
Martian maths - Martian maths
Martian mathematics...

The square root of 11
Is 12 times 1.8
If a biscuit costs you 50p
How much for a chocolate cake (with a flake)

5 times 2 is a triangle
Minus six is green
X plus y is a kangaroo
Which equals an ice cream (in your dreams)

Martian maths - Martian maths
Martian maths..... is totally daft
Martian maths - Martian maths
Martian mathematics.....

Pink Fluffy Unicorn

Pink fluffy unicorn
With an ice cream on it's head,
Choked on a rainbow
Now it is dead.

When Mr Beezley Sneezes

When Mr Beezley sneezes we always try to hide
When Mr Beezley sneezes he's most undignified
When Mr Beezley sneezes he splatters every side
His eyes start to itch
His nose starts to twitch
And his mouth does this
As he goes...

Aah ... Aah ... ATCHOOO!
Bless you

When Mr Beezley sneezes it's like a river rushing
When Mr Beezley sneezes it's green and it is gushing
When Mr Beezley sneezes it's like a toilet flushing
His eyes start to itch
His nose starts to twitch
And his mouth does this
As he goes...

Aah ... Aah ... ATCHOOO!
Bless you

When Mr Beezley sneezes I wish he'd warn and tell us
When Mr Beezley sneezes an elephant would be jealous
When Mr Beezley sneezes we all need umbrellas
His eyes start to itch
His nose starts to twitch
And his mouth does this
As he goes ...

Aah ... Aah ... ATCHOOO!
Bless you

School Trip

School trip, it's a cool trip
Flying in our rocket ship
School trip, it's a cool trip
Flying in our rocket ship

We want to go on a day trip
Somewhere that is ace
Flying in a rocket ship
Into outer space

We want to go to a theme park
With lots of rocket rides
Thrills and spills and tracks and wheels
Churning our insides

We want to meet the milky way
Dance to the distant beats
And see a supernova
With popcorn, drinks and treats

We want to fly to the countryside
Higher than the sky
To see the Earth beneath our feet
As it rolls on by

We want to go on a day trip
Somewhere that is ace
Flying our own rocket ship
Into outer space

We want to go - to the moon
Where no-one else can reach us
But most of all we want to go
To a place without any teachers!

School trip, it's a cool trip
Flying in our rocket ship
School trip, it's a cool trip
Flying in our rocket ship

Can You Guess Where Teachers Keep Their Pets?

Mr Spratt has got a cat. Sleeps beneath his bobble hat
Mrs Cox has got a fox. Nesting in her sweaty socks
Mr Spry has Fred the fly. Living on his favourite tie

Then there's Mr Spare. Poor old Mr Spare.
He's got a grizzly bear. Living in his under...

Mrs Groat has got a stoat. On the collar of her coat
Miss Cahoots has lots of newts. Living in her zip up boots
Mr Monk has 13 skunks. Living in his swimming trunks

Then there's Mr Chance. Poor old Mr Chance.
He has got a thousand ants. Living in his under...

Mr Best has got a nest. Of giant bees in his vest
Mrs Big – has got a twig. Living in her ginger wig
Mrs Black has got a yak. Living in her anorak.

Then there's Mrs Vickers. Poor old Mrs Vickers.
She has got a stick insect. Living in her .... handbag.

Tricks to play on teachers

Trick No. 3 - for the Headteacher ...

On our headteacher's
Special day
We made a birthday cake
With curried beans
And mouldy greens
To make their stomach ache
We slipped some mice in
To the icing
Brushed it with a rotten egg
Then added snails
And fingernails
To make a perfect cake for our head.

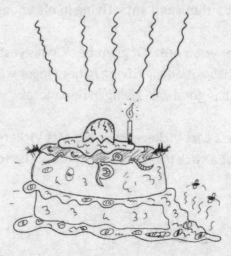

Bouncy Mr Springer

He bounces when he walks
He bounces when he talks
You can tell where he has been
He's a human trampoline

He bounces in assembly
His rubber knees are trembly
He bounces out of the classroom door
Bounces down the corridor

Bouncy Mr Springer

Boing, boing, ba-doing, boing, boing
Boing, boing, ba-doing, boing, boing

I think when he was small
He swallowed a ping pong ball
You can tell where he has been
He's a human trampoline

You sometimes get the feeling
He could bounce off the ceiling
He bounces out of the classroom door
Bounces down the corridor

Bouncy Mr Springer.

Boing, boing, ba-doing, boing, boing
Boing, boing, ba-doing, boing, boing

He bounces every single day
Bounces when he does ballet
When he bounces you will too
Cos he's human kangaroo

He bounced when he was small
It helped him grow so tall
His dad is bouncy, so is mum
That's why he has such a bouncy ... bum

Bouncy Mr Springer.

Boing, boing, ba-doing, boing, boing
Boing, boing, ba-doing, boing, boing

Huge, Hungry Crocodile

One day I won't forget,
Is the day that I met
A huge, hungry crocodile
Floating down the river Nile   SNAP.
Sharp teeth, sharp claws
Strong tail, strong jaws   SNAP.

Thought that he
Might eat me up
But then he gave me
A paper cup
Of orange juice
Tasty orange juice SLURP

I drank my juice
Floating down the river
Then the crocodile
Invited me to dinner
Dinner? What a winner
He invited me to dinner
A huge, hungry crocodile
Floating down the river Nile SNAP

The crocodile was hungry
He was ready to eat
Said that what he wanted
Was fresh juicy meat
Fresh juicy meat?
Ready to eat?   UH OH

We got to his house
The cupboard was bare
He invited me to dinner
But no *food* was there
No food anywhere
No food was there   UH OH.

Crocodile licked his lips   SLURP
Oh no, could it be?
The fresh juicy meat he wanted
Might just be me
Fresh and juicy
Good enough to eat
That might just be me   UH OH

A huge, hungry crocodile
Floating down the river Nile   SNAP
Sharp teeth, sharp claws
Strong tail, strong jaws   SNAP

Crocodile opened up the oven   UH OH
Told me to climb inside   UH OH
Put my head inside the oven   UH OH
Couldn't believe my eyes   PHEW
It was filled with sausages, burgers and pies
SIGH
He didn't want to eat me
He was just being friendly   PHEW

That is why I won't forget
The special day, that I met
A huge, hungry crocodile
Floating down the river Nile   SNAP
Sharp teeth, sharp claws
Strong tail, strong jaws   SNAP

The crocodile and me are now best friends
And this is how the story ends
Me and the crocodile
Floating down the river Nile
Best of friends   SIGH
Best of friends   UH OH

SNAP!

Not on Your Nelly

Do you want a shark in your swimming pool?
Not on your Nelly
Do you think your teachers look so cool?
Not on your Nelly
Do you want a cactus on your chair?
A hedgehog in your underwear?
Or a ferret nesting in your hair?
Not on your Nelly

Nelly - Nelly - who is this Nelly?
It rhymes with belly and it rhymes with jelly
It rhymes with telly and it rhymes with smelly
But who on earth is Nelly?

Do you want homework for 10 years?
Not on your Nelly
Do you want spiders in your ears?
Not on your Nelly
Do you want a beetle in your bed?
Brussel sprouts on mouldy bread?
Or smelly cabbage salad instead?
Not on your Nelly

Nelly - Nelly - who is this Nelly?
It rhymes with belly and it rhymes with jelly
It rhymes with telly and it rhymes with smelly
But who on earth is Nelly?

Is she the girl with a big fat belly?
Is she the girl who likes to eat jelly?
Does she read the news on the telly?
Is she the Gran whose feet are smelly?
Does she like to shop at the deli?
Buying lots of tagliatelli?
Is she selling vermicelli?
Who on earth is Nelly?

Nelly - Nelly - who is this Nelly?
It rhymes with belly and it rhymes with jelly
It rhymes with telly and it rhymes with smelly
But who on earth is Nelly?

Do you want to clean your room?
Not on your Nelly
Go to bed far too soon?
Not on your Nelly
Do you want to shave an orang utan?
Wrestle a sumo from Japan?
Or even get a kiss from a man called Stan?
NOT ON YOUR NELLY.

Nelly - Nelly - who is this Nelly?
It rhymes with belly and it rhymes with jelly
It rhymes with telly and it rhymes with smelly
But who on earth is Nelly?

Ssh, Ssh, Left and Right

Ssh, ssh, left and right
Ssh, ssh, out of sight

Shoes
Silver shoes
Shiny silver shoes
Soft shiny, silver shoes
Soft soled, shiny silver, shoes

Gliding down the corridor
Sliding on the slippy floor
Doing nothing by the door
Who are they waiting for?

Ssh, ssh, left and right
Ssh, ssh, out of sight

Super scary,
Slightly slippy,
Simply silent,
Never skippy.

Gliding down the corridor
Sliding on the slippy floor
Doing nothing by the door
Who are they waiting for?

Ssh, ssh, left and right
Ssh, ssh, out of sight.

Shoes
(news)
Silver shoes
(bad news)
Shiny silver shoes
(big, bad news)
Soft shiny, silver shoes
(bringing big, bad news)
Soft soled, shiny silver, shoes
(here they come now)

Ssh, ssh, left and right
Ssh, ssh, out of sight.

BOO!

Dirty, Filthy – Lies

I love telling stories, think that I know why
All my favourite stories, are dirty, filthy – lies.

All my favourite stories, are

DIRTY

FILTHY

LIES!

Here is a story, the sort that you can sing,
If you're sitting comfortably, I will begin...

Once upon a time
I swam up to the moon
Met a happy alien
We sang a happy tune.

We had sandwiches for dinner
Sandwiches for tea
When I tried to leave
He made a sandwich out of me!

I love telling stories, think that I know why
All my favourite stories, are dirty, filthy – lies.

All my favourite stories, are

           DIRTY

                  FILTHY

                        LIES!

Here's another story, this one might be true
If you're sitting comfortably, I'll tell it to you...

In a land far away
There's a zombie called Mike
He's big and he's strong
But he's not very bright.

He walks around all day
With his brain in a box
It's not in his head
Because his head fell off.

I love telling stories, think that I know why
All my favourite stories, are dirty, filthy – lies.

All my favourite stories, are

           DIRTY

                  FILTHY

                        LIES!

When You Read

You can do anything
You can go anywhere
All you need is a book
And your favourite comfy chair
Satisfaction guaranteed
When …. you … READ!

You can sit beside a spider
Eat ice cream with a chimpanzee
You can kiss a kangaroo
Take a tiger home for tea
You can dance with a donkey
Wear a carrot on your head
Eat slimy eyeballs
Keep a dragon in your bed
Satisfaction guaranteed
When …. you … READ!

You can drive a racing car
Eats lots of sweets
You can score the winning goal,
Every day of the week
You can rule the world
Have diamonds in your hair
You can be a crazy alien - or
Be a billionaire

You can do anything
You can go anywhere
All you need is a book
And your favourite comfy chair

Satisfaction guaranteed
When …. you … READ!

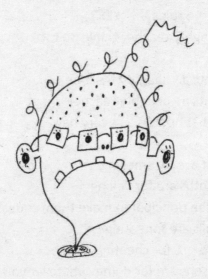

Naughty Teacher

Nobody wants a - naughty teacher
Nobody wants a - naughty teacher
Cos this is what he says …. every day

> A can is for kicking
> Kids are for tricking
> Homework is work you don't have to do
> School time is boring
> Rules are for ignoring
> Lessons are time to take a snooze

Do you think that's cool?   YES
Being bad at school?   YES
Breaking all the rules?   YES
Well, the naughty teacher thinks so too!

Nobody wants a - naughty teacher
Nobody wants a - naughty teacher
Cos this is what he says …. every day

> Feet are for smelling
> Mouths are for yelling
> At the principal to make them squeal
> Snails are for eating
> Tests are for cheating
> Lessons are for doing, whatever you feel.

Do you think that's cool?   YES
Being bad at school?   YES
Breaking all the rules?   YES
Well, the naughty teacher thinks so too!

Nobody wants a - naughty teacher
Nobody wants a - naughty teacher
Cos this is what he says …. every day

Do you think that's cool?   YES
Being bad at school?   YES
Breaking all the rules?   YES
Would you like a naughty teacher too?

What do you want? (a naughty teacher)
What do you really want? (a naughty teacher)
What do you really, really, really want?

A NAUGHTY TEACHER!!!

DIY Poems

DIY - in other words,
"Do it yourself"
Is exciting, enjoyable and good for your health.

DIY birthday cards,
Made by hand,
Are the best birthday cards in the land.

DIY biscuits,
Buns or sweets,
Are the tastiest treats you can eat.

DIY poetry,
Allows you to say,
Exactly what you're feeling today.

Which is why
You may find,
DIY poems are a bit strange, sometimes.

If I Could Choose

If I could choose the gifts
That life would give to me
What choices would I make
And just who would I be?

I wouldn't choose fast cars
Being friends with all the stars
I wouldn't choose to sign an autograph
I wouldn't choose to rule the sky
Be superman or to fly
I wouldn't choose to cry - when I could laugh

I wouldn't choose fame
People calling out my name
I wouldn't choose pots and pots of money
I wouldn't choose to be the best
Or be brighter than the rest
Although I wouldn't mind being funny

I wouldn't choose football
Or any sport at all
I wouldn't choose big muscles for a fight
I wouldn't choose pride of place
Or to have the prettiest face
I wouldn't choose the wrong - instead of right

If I could choose the gifts
That life could give to me,
I'd choose good friends, good health
And ... my family

But win or lose
I would choose
To just
      be
         ME.

Let No-one Steal Your Dreams

Let no-one steal your dreams
Let no-one tear apart
The fires of ambition
That burn inside your heart

Let no-one steal your dreams
Follow your heart, follow your soul
For only when you follow them
Will you feel truly whole

Set yours sights and keep them fixed
Set your sights on high
Let no-one steal your dreams from you
Your only limit is the sky

Let no-one steal your dreams
Let no-one tell you that you can't believe.
Let no-one hold you back
Let no-one tell you that you won't achieve

Let no-one steal your dreams
Follow your heart, follow your soul
For only when you follow them
Will you feel truly whole

Set yours sights and keep them fixed
Set your sights on high
Let no-one steal your dreams
Your only limit is the sky

Let no-one steal your dreams

We are The Writers

It only takes one spark to start the fire
Just one idea to inspire
It only takes one dream to take you higher

So many writers

It only takes one voice to breathe these words
So they live and so they can be heard
These lines and these rhymes will give the world

So many writers

We are readers, we are writers
We love to share the words that excite us

We are the writers.

A short history of Stan Cullimore .

When Stan was young, he dreamed of being a mathematics teacher. Which is a bit strange, to be honest. He went to Hull University to follow his dream and then something even stranger happened. He became a popstar. By accident.

Which is pretty strange when you think about it. His band was called The Housemartins and they sold millions of records worldwide. Which was very nice.

Later on, Stan got married to his (lovely) wife and these days they have four fantastic children, six superb grandchildren and a very friendly dog. Along the way, Stan remembered that he loved telling stories.

So he started writing books. He also began writing and appearing in TV shows. The last time he checked, Stan found he had written 127 books for children as well as countless songs, poems and TV episodes. Which seems like quite a lot, to my way of thinking.

These days Stan writes articles for newspapers and magazines. He also travels the globe with his favourite ukulele, performing his works and leading workshops for students of all ages. Getting students, teachers and everyone else to join in performing poems, singing songs, laughing lots and writing creative masterpieces. It's always great fun!

If you would like this world famous author, musician, poet and storyteller to visit your school, go to his website:
<u>www.stancullimore.com</u>

A Short History of Paul Cookson

When Paul was young he wanted to be a footballer. When he realised he wasn't good enough to be a footballer, he decided to be a pop star. Then he remembered that he couldn't sing or play guitar. Or anything.

So, he became a teacher instead and spent a lot of his spare time writing poems. Lots of them. Eventually, twenty eight years ago, Paul stopped teaching and became a poet.

Since then he has visited thousands of schools to perform his work, lead workshops and generally make people laugh. He has also written and edited over fifty books - including the best selling *The Works.* Currently, he has sold well over a million books.

One of his jobs is the official Poet In Residence for The National Football Museum. Also Noddy Holder said he is Slade's Poet's Laureate - so it must be true.

Ten years ago his wife bought him a ukulele for Christmas and she has regretted it ever since. He now has ten of them (including three electric ones) and has learnt almost ten chords (including three difficult ones). He even knows the names of a few of the chords.

Sometimes, Paul sends his poems to Stan, who completely changes them by turning them into songs.

If you'd like him to visit your school you can contact him through his website : www.paulcooksonpoet.co.uk